Hello Kitty

HAPPY VALENTINE'S DAY

By Elizabeth Bennett
Illustrated by Sachiho Hino

SCHOLASTIC INC.

New York   Toronto   London   Auckland   Sydney
Mexico City   New Delhi   Hong Kong   Buenos Aires

Decorate the pictures in this book with stickers. The page numbers on the sticker pages will help you figure out which stickers to use.

ISBN O-439-79110-3

All rights reserved. Published by Scholastic Inc., 557 Broadway, New York, NY 10012. SCHOLASTIC and associated logos are trademarks and/or registered trademarks of Scholastic Inc.

12 11 10 9 8 7 6 5 4 3 2 1   6 7 8 9 10 11/0

Printed in the U.S.A.
First printing, January 2006

Hello Kitty couldn't wait!
Valentine's Day was just two days away.
Her class was having a big party with red
heart cookies and pink lemonade.

Today, everyone was going to make special valentine mailboxes.
Then, on Friday, they would bring in valentines to deliver to their friends.

"I hope I get lots and lots of valentines!"
said Hello Kitty.
"Me, too!" said Fifi.

Hello Kitty and Kathy decorated
their mailboxes with hearts.
Fifi put flowers on hers.

Joey colored his mailbox with red and white stripes.
Tippy painted his with polka dots.

When Hello Kitty got home from school,
she started making valentines.
First Hello Kitty folded a piece of red
paper in half.

Then she drew an outline on the paper.
When she cut it out and opened it, she
had a heart!

Hello Kitty made a beautiful red heart for everyone in her class.
She decorated the red hearts with smaller pink hearts, stickers, and glitter.

Then she wrote, "Happy Valentine's Day!
Love, Hello Kitty."

On Friday, Hello Kitty woke up early.
Valentine's Day was here!

At breakfast, there were valentines for Hello
Kitty and Mimmy from Mama and Papa.
"Thank you," called Hello Kitty as she ran
to the bus stop.

13

At school, Hello Kitty delivered a valentine
to each of her friends' mailboxes.

She even had one for Mr. Bearly.

After art class, everyone checked their
mailboxes.
"I got a valentine!" said Fifi.

16

"I got one, too!" cried Tracy.
"So did I," said Joey.

Hello Kitty looked in her mailbox.
It was empty!
She looked under the mailbox.

She looked in her cubby.
But she didn't find any valentines!

After lunch, Hello Kitty looked in her
mailbox again.
It was still empty.

*I wonder where all my valentines are,
she thought. Did my friends forget
about me?*

At two o'clock, the valentine's party started.
"Yummy! I love heart-shaped cookies," said Tracy.

"You love *any*-shaped cookies." Tippy laughed.
Then Mr. Bearly told the class it was time to open their valentines.

Everyone was so excited.
"I got ten valentines!" said Joey.

"Look how pretty this one is," said Fifi.
Hello Kitty just sat quietly.

Then Kathy opened up her mailbox.
It was filled to the top!

She took out a valentine.
"This one has your name on it,
Hello Kitty," said Kathy.

Kathy took out another valentine.
"And so does this one!"

Kathy emptied her mailbox onto her desk.

Half of the valentines were for Kathy.
And half were for Hello Kitty!

"Our mailboxes look so much alike. Your valentines were delivered to *me*!" Kathy laughed.

Hello Kitty smiled.
She was so happy. Her friends *hadn't*
forgotten about her!
"Happy Valentine's Day to everyone!"
she said.